The Don't-give-up Kid

AND LEARNING DIFFERENCES

The Don't-give-up Kid

AND LEARNING DIFFERENCES

BY JEANNE GEHRET, M.A.
Illustrations and design by Sandra Ann DePauw

Verbal Images Press
Fairport, New York

The author wishes to thank the following people who served as consultants on this book:

Francis Bennett, Ph.D., Clinical Developmental Psychologist; **Roberta Beyer**, Assistant Superintendent of Schools, Penfield, New York; **Patricia Bourcy**, Training Specialist, City School District of Rochester; **Kathryn Cappella,** Association for the Learning Disabled of Genesee Valley; **Jayne Gifford**, Executive Director, Camp Fire, Rochester/Monroe County; **Bernie Kumetat, M.D.**, Child Psychiatrist; **Virginia McHugh**, Administrator, Montessori School of Rochester; **Daniel Nussbaum II, M.D.**, Genesee Developmental Center

ISBN 1-884281-10-9 softcover
ISBN 1-884281-15-x hardcover
Second edition © 1996 Jeanne Gehret, M.A.
Second edition illustrations © 1996 Sandra Ann DePauw

Printed in the United States of America
First printing: February 1990
Second printing: May 1991
Third printing: November 1991
Fourth printing: December 1992
Fifth printing: February 1995
Sixth printing: November 1995

Cataloging-in-Publication Data
Gehret, Jeanne.
  The don't-give-up kid and learning differences / by Jeanne Gehret ; illustrations and design by Sandra Ann DePauw.
  p. cm.
  Includes bibliographical references.
  SUMMARY: As Alex becomes aware of his different learning style, he realizes his hero Thomas Edison had similar problems. Together they try new solutions until they succeed at their dream to create things that no one ever thought of before.
  ISBN 1-884281-10-9 (pbk.)
  ISBN 1-884281-15-x (hbk.)
  1. Learning ability--Juvenile fiction. 2. Learning--Methods--Juvenile fiction. I. DePauw, Sandra A. II. Title
LB1134.G4 1990   808.89'9282   QBI91-1853

Verbal Images Press
19 Fox Hill Drive • Fairport, New York 14450
(716) 377-3807 • Fax (716) 377-5401

To my Don't-give-up Kid:
may all of your dreams come true

My name is Alex. But Mom calls me the Don't-give-up Kid because I keep finding new ways to ask the same question.

I want to be a famous inventor like Thomas Edison, the man who invented light bulbs. And I've been working on some inventions of my own.

Before I can become an inventor, though, Dad says I have to learn to read and behave in school. And when it comes to school, I stop being the Don't-give-up Kid. That's because school is where everything goes wrong.

And I mean *everything*.

Here's what happened on one of my worst days.

Before school Mrs. Potter, my teacher, asked me to help her unpack some new books. Holding them together was a giant rubber band — just what I needed for the chopper I was making. I took it to my desk.

Then I looked up. Mrs. Potter was standing by my desk, and the other kids were standing for Opening Exercises. She took my rubber band and said I could have it back at the end of the day.

After Opening Exercises, it started to rain outside. I wondered if I could invent a bubble big enough to keep me dry. I started to draw bubbles on my book.

"Alex, your turn to read," said Mrs. Potter. Everyone was watching me. I couldn't find the place for the longest time. Then she walked over to my desk and said, "Alex, put down your pencil and pay attention." She pointed to where I was supposed to read.

I stared at my book. Had I ever seen those letters before? The words seemed to jump around the page. Some looked backwards. Nobody made a sound while I tried to figure out what it said.

Then I began to read slowly so I could get every word right. "My hat is on pot of my head," I said. The boy behind me put his head down and started to laugh. Soon the whole class was laughing with him.

"On *top*, Alex," said Mrs. Potter. "Not *on pot.*"

I don't like to read, even at home. Dad said I just have to try harder. "Come on, Alex. I've read *Edison the Inventor* to you lots of times. Now let's read it together."

I asked him if we could play checkers instead.

One day Mom asked me if I'd like to have a friend over.

"How about that nice boy who sits next to you? What's his name?" she asked.

"Mark," I answered. But Mark wasn't nice. He made fun of me when I said "dead" instead of "bed." I felt like crawling under my desk so he couldn't look at me anymore.

"Well, how about Mark?" she asked.

"I don't think so," I replied, and turned away.

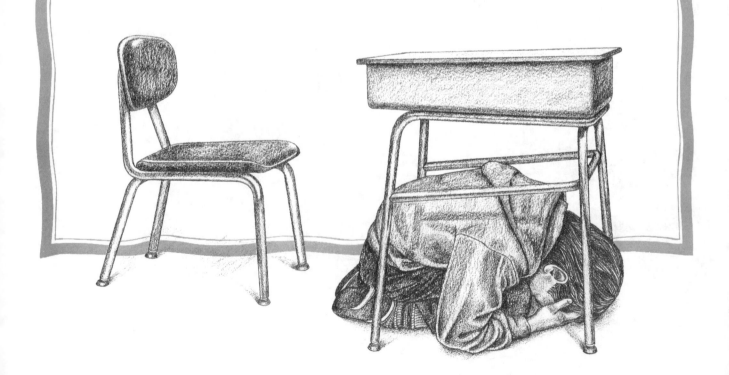

A few days after that, Mom took me to see Dr. Powell, who is a psychologist. He's not like my other doctor who gives me shots and checks my eyes. Instead, he asked me to tell him about the pictures in his book and connect the dots on his drawings.

Then he wanted to know about school. I told him how hard it is to read and stay out of trouble.

"I guess I'm just stupid," I said.

Later Mom sat on my bed to talk. "Alex," she said, "Dr. Powell told us why you're having trouble in school. You're very smart, but he said you learn in a different way from other children.

"When most people read, the letters stay in one place on the page, but for you they jump around.

"Most kids can pay attention when there are many things to look at. But you see everything at once. It's hard for you to concentrate."

She looked right into my eyes. "Would you like to do better in school?"

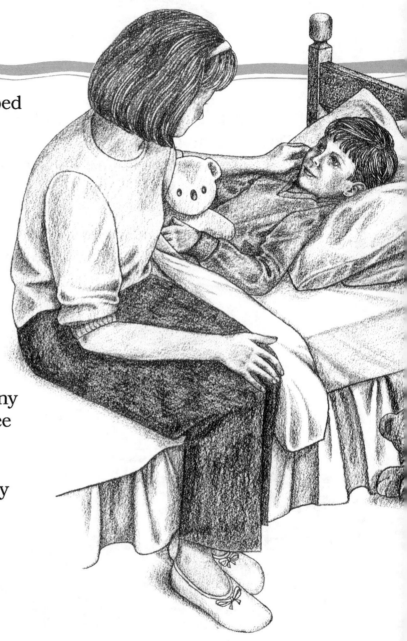

I stared at my favorite blanket. "No."

"Why not, Alex? I thought you were the Don't-give-up Kid." She winked at me, but her smile was sad.

"Because I can't!" I said, trying not to cry. "I try so hard, but I still can't read. And I'm always doing the wrong thing!"

"When you want something at home, Alex," Mom said, "you know how you keep trying one thing after another until I say yes?" I nodded. "Kids who learn differently need to try new ways to learn. I talked to the principal and they're going to let you work with Mrs. Baxter. She'll help you find your special way to learn."

And that's when things began to get better.

Mrs. Baxter's room is different. It's smaller and quieter than my regular class, so I can concentrate better. Best of all, Mrs. Baxter spends a lot of time with me. She makes me feel really special.

At first, I was afraid she'd give me long books that I couldn't read. And that she'd think I was stupid. But she didn't.

Instead, Mrs. Baxter gave me a card with just one word on it: run. Then another card: sun. With only one word on each card, I could put the letters back together pretty quickly if they jumped around.

Another card: bun. Or was it gun?

She waited. I didn't want to make a mistake, so I didn't answer.

Then she told me a story about Thomas Edison, the inventor. One of his inventions took 10,000 tries before it would work.

One day he was asked, "How does it feel to have failed 10,000 times?"

"I didn't fail 10,000 times," Mr. Edison answered. "I succeeded at finding 10,000 ways that don't work." After many more tries, his invention was a big success.

If I want to be like Mr. Edison, I have to keep trying too.

"Come on, Alex, don't give up," I said to myself, and concentrated hard on the word in front of me.

"B-un," I read slowly.

Mrs. Baxter nodded and gave me another card to read. I felt really good.

Since then, I've done lots of reading with her. She makes it fun. If I finish my work ahead of time, she lets me play checkers with the other kids.

All the kids who work with Mrs. Baxter have a learning difference. That means some kinds of learning are hard for us. She says we're not stupid; we just need to find our own ways to learn.

Shelly has trouble remembering what she *hears*. She never used to follow directions. Now she can, because Mrs. Baxter writes things down for her.

Jonathan has trouble writing, even though he can read. So now when he takes a test, he tells the teacher the answers and she writes them for him. Otherwise he'd never finish writing.

It's hard for Michael to say what he's thinking, and people used to call him stupid. But he can *write* just fine — much better than I can.

My parents told me that nobody knows how kids get learning differences. You can't catch them, like a cold. Some people think you're born with them.

Sometimes I work with Shelly and Michael and Jonathan. They don't laugh when I make mistakes. Michael even came to my birthday party.

Some kids need special ways to learn, just like other kids need help for other things.

My sister Kate is five and she still needs training wheels on her bike. Otherwise she loses her balance and falls off.

You should see her knees!

My neighbor Kerri has to wear braces. Her teeth are too big for her mouth.

I think my cousin Sarah has the worst problem of all, though — she has to get shots every month or she sneezes all the time.

Even a Don't-give-up Kid wants to quit when the going gets tough. But if something's important to you, I guess you just have to keep working at it till you get it right.

Mrs. Baxter won't let me give up on reading. Thanks to her, I can read better now.

Now I can read cereal boxes. And street signs as we drive to the store.

And every night Dad reads to me from the book about Thomas Edison. Did you know that Mr. Edison had trouble writing? Maybe he had a learning difference, too.

Dad said many famous people have learning differences. Some have made famous statues and paintings. One was governor of New York. Others have become singers and actors. And another won the Olympics!

These people had trouble learning, but they kept trying. And their learning problems didn't keep them from doing other things very well.

12 FT

I can swim really fast. I can do my cousin's math, even though he's two years older than I am. And I can make things that no one ever thought of before. So I'm not going to let my problems with reading make me feel bad about myself anymore.

Someday I'll read that Thomas Edison book all by myself. But first I want to try out my latest invention: a propeller, made with giant rubber bands, to wear on my back and make me fly.

And if that doesn't work, I'll just strap on some helium balloons.

Talking to Kids About LD: Guidelines for Caring Adults

When the first edition of this book was published in 1990, I called it *Learning Disabilities And The Don't-give-up Kid*. Later, I changed its title to reflect educational theorists' suggestion that many so-called learning *disabilities* are better described as *different ways of learning*. Thinking of youngsters as different, rather than disabled, changes what we tell them about themselves and how we treat them.

Should We Tell Children They Have LD?

Consider this discussion that arose between a father and a school counselor after a child was formally classified as having a learning disability:

> *"One last thing, Mr. Curtis," said the counselor. "If I were you, I wouldn't tell Molly she has a learning disability." The girl's father looked puzzled.*
>
> *"Many children give up when they hear they have a disability," explained the counselor."Molly may begin to feel she's no good at anything, even at subjects where she's strong. Or she may use the learning disability to get extra help in areas where she doesn't need it. She might develop a poor self-image."*
>
> *"But it wouldn't be fair to keep it from her," the father objected. "Molly thinks she's stupid because she works twice as hard as her friends for half the results. If I don't tell her that a different learning style is responsible for some of her failures, she'll continue to have this distorted view of herself. And that's what I call a poor self-image!"*

They're both right. Telling children they have a learning disability (LD) may mislead them into thinking they can't learn at all. But witholding the information keeps them from adapting successfully to their uniqueness. My solution: tell children that they have a learning difference, and use the term disability with educators who need it to deliver special services.

When handled properly, discussing different learning styles with youngsters can help them to reinterpret past failures, cooperate with educational modifications, and find new avenues to success.

Acknowledging Differences Brings Relief

Parents of newly-diagnosed children often report an odd sense of relief that their youngsters' failures are caused by biological differences rather than bad parenting. They gain comfort, as well as practical suggestions, from attending support groups and meeting other families with the problem.

It's the same with educators. Once a learning disorder has been identified in a particular child, teachers weed out ineffective instructional methods and replace them with new ones that work.

For adults, knowledge is power. So why should it be any different for children? Like adults, youngsters feel relief when they realize that their failures stem from something they don't cause. They take comfort from learning about other LD sufferers who have succeeded. And when they are asked to work with a different teacher or try a new "learning game," they are more willing because they understand why.

So *how* do we tell them? Find a time when the child is calm and not occupied with other activities. Remind him of recent difficulties in school. "You know how hard it is for you to read? Remember the night you recited your spelling list perfectly, then failed thetest on it the next day?"

Then borrow some ideas from the mother in this book as she talks to her young son about his learning style:

- Tell the child that his difficulties are caused by the way his brain works, and that the problem is not his fault.
- Explain that he is not retarded, no matter what others may say. (A person who is retarded does not have the intelligence to progress beyond a certain point. A person with a learning disability, however, can progress if he can get around his particular stumbling block.) For this reason, tell the child, you prefer to use the expression *learning difference.*
- Emphasize that he can overcome these difficulties by using different ways to learn, and that he will receive plenty of help.

That's probably enough for the first session. As time goes by, reinforce that initial conversation with further discussion:

- Read stories together about real-life heroes who have overcome a variety of barriers such as poverty, racism, gender bias, and physical challenges. This will help him identify with role models who achieved success through hard work.

- Identify and explain your child's specific weakness. For example, "You have a problem with putting your thoughts into written words. You know what you mean, but by the time the words get to your hand they're all mixed up and come out wrong." Then link these difficulties with new learning strategies like this: "That's why you're going to learn to use a computer. Many people with this problem find typing easier than handwriting. You can even type thank-you notes to Grandma after Christmas."
- Help the child write his own "Don't-give-up Kid" story, mentioning both his difficulty and his strength. Encourage him to share it with caring adults and maybe even friends.

Explore Multiple Intelligences to Turn Differences Into Strengths

A child who exhibits flashes of brilliance despite school problems often prompts adults to ask, "How can she do so poorly in school, when I *know* she's smart?" Recent writings about multiple intelligences by Howard Gardner and others why this question is often asked about youngsters with LD. Although humans have seven ways of knowing (types of intelligence), traditional education focuses primarily on the two that dominate standard achievement tests:

- Mathematical/logical—scientific reasoning; performing complex calculations; recognizing abstract patterns; and
- Verbal/linguistic—learning and expressing through written and spoken words; remembering and recalling concepts through words.

In addition to these mathematical and verbal abilities, people also have five other kinds of intelligence as described in *Seven Ways of Knowing,* by David Lazear:

- Visual/spatial—finding one's way in space; drawing, making mental pictures;
- Musical/rhythmic—creating melody and rhythm; understanding the structure of music and sound;
- Bodily/kinesthetic—exploring through touch and movement; expressing through spontaneous or planned movements;
- Interpersonal—understanding people's intentions and behaviors; perceiving from someone else's experience; working cooperatively in a group;
- Intrapersonal—reflecting on one's own experiences; making appropriate choices; understanding and expressing personal feelings.

LD youngsters often learn better through, and even excel in, some of the not-so-prominent areas of intelligence. In fact, those who have become happy adults report a point at which they began to associate themselves more with their many talents than with their few weaknesses. (See article by Mark Katz, Ph.D. cited below.) By broadening traditional education to include all seven learning styles, we can greatly improve LD children's chances for success once they leave school. Here are some places to begin:

- Observe their habits and areas of competence, especially those outside of the verbal or mathematical areas. If they move around constantly while trying to listen, perhaps they learn through the bodily/kinesthetic channel. If they love rhyming stories like Dr. Seuss or hum to themselves, they may learn through the musical/rhythmic intelligence.
- Take a break from graded academic projects to introduce such children to the other forms of intelligence. Help them explore their special strengths through activities like martial arts, painting, music, theater, and religious expression. A word of caution: When you want youngsters to try new things, focus on the enjoyable process rather than pushing them to produce a finished product.
- Help students to learn through their preferred style. In school, offer alternative methods for both acquiring information and communicating what is understood. Perhaps you are dealing with a child with language deficits and a preference for visual learning. Allow her to demonstrate her understanding of a Social Studies unit by creating a map, graph, or diorama and explaining (orally) what it means. Encourage a youngster with a low aptitude for abstract mathematics to learn multiplication and division facts by grouping and counting coins.

In *Creating Minds,* Gardner points out that geniuses usually have close confidants who offer both emotional and intellectual support. Sally Smith in her book *Succeeding Against The Odds* reports that most successful adults with LD report having had at least one caring childhood mentor. That person admired and helped them develop their strengths, dried their tears, and encouraged them to go on.

Are you the parent, teacher, neighbor, coach, relative, or friend of a child with a learning difference? Then that significant, caring adult may very well be you.

Jeanne Gehret

PARENT RESOURCE GUIDE

A list of the specific learning differences described in
The Don't-give-up Kid:

(* indicates a character from this book)

- **auditory processing** - difficulty understanding what one hears, or problems distinguishing between different sounds. Shelly* has a problem with auditory processing.
- **dyslexia** - problems remembering and recognizing written letters, numbers, and words; may result in backwards reading or poor handwriting. Alex* has dyslexia.
- **dysgraphia** - difficulty expressing thoughts through writing. Jonathan* has dysgraphia.
- **expressive language disability** - difficulty expressing oneself through speech. Michael* has an expressive language disability.

People with learning disabilities may also have problems with:

- **attention** - inability to focus on relevant information, screen out distractions, or stay on task. Alex* has attention problems because of his learning disabilities. Some children with Attention Deficit Disorder may have attention problems *without* learning disabilities.
- **memory** - difficulties remembering things that happened a short or long time ago.
- **sequencing** - knowing and carrying through procedures in a particular order.
- **visual perception** - difficulty distinguishing one visual element from another.

For more information, contact:

- Your local school district's Committee on Special Education (also called Child Study Team)
- Learning Disabilities Association of America, 4156 Library Road, Pittsburgh, PA 15234**
- Orton Dyslexia Society, 724 York Road, Baltimore, MD 21204**

**Look for state and local chapters of these organizations

Bibliography For Talking to Kids About LD:

Books:

Davis, Ronald. *The Gift of Dyslexia.* Burlingame, California: Ability Workshop, 1994.

Gardner, Howard. *Creating Minds: An Anatomy of Creativity Seen Through the Lives of Freud, Einstein, Picasso, Stravinsky, Eliot, Graham, and Gandhi.* New York: Basic Books, 1993.

--------------------- *Frames of Mind: The Theory of Multiple Intelligences.* New York: Basic Books, 1983.

Lazear, David. *Seven Ways of Knowing: Teaching for the Multiple Intelligences.* Palatine, Illinois: Skylight Publications, 1981.

Parzych, Holly. *Why Are You Calling Me LD?* Freeport, Illinois: Peekan Publications, 1989.

Smith, Sally L. *Succeeding Against The Odds: Strategies and Insights from the Learning Disabled.* Los Angeles: J. P. Tarcher, 1992.

Webb, James T., Elizabeth A. Meckstroth and Stephanie S. Tolan. *Guiding the Gifted Child.* Dayton, Ohio: Ohio Psychology, 1982.

Articles:

Baum, Susan. *Gifted But Learning Disabled: A Puzzling Paradox.* ERIC Digest, 1990 (E479).

Katz, Mark, Ph.D. "From Challenged Childhood to Achieving Adulthood: Studies in Resilience." *CHADDer,* May 1994: 8-11.

ALSO BY JEANNE GEHRET:

Eagle Eyes: A Child's Guide to Paying Attention
Explains ADD from the perspective of a child who has it.
Picture book for ages 6 to 10.

I'm Somebody Too
Eagle Eyes' sister tells how it feels to have a brother with ADD.
Novel for ages 9 and up.

Susan B. Anthony And Justice For All
Biography of the famous reformer who overcame sexism and slavery.
Ages 9 and up.

NEW! ASK ABOUT:

Teacher Handbook on I'm Somebody Too
Reproducible workbook applying the multiple-intelligences approach to
teach reading and writing, acceptance of differences, and more.

Special Reports
Short, concise articles on hard-to-find specifics about the daily
challenges of coping with differences.

Verbal Images Press
19 Fox Hill Drive • Fairport, New York 14450
(716) 377-3807 • Fax (716) 377-5401